FEYNMAN'S PROMISE

Amrita Mukherjee

AuthorHouse™
1663 Liberty Drive
Bloomington, IN 47403
www.authorhouse.com
Phone: 1 (800) 839-8640

Published by AuthorHouse   06/30/2017

ISBN: 978-1-5246-9794-5 (sc)
ISBN: 978-1-5246-9795-2 (e)

Library of Congress Control Number: 2017910123

Print information available on the last page.

Any people depicted in stock imagery provided by Thinkstock are models,
and such images are being used for illustrative purposes only.
Certain stock imagery © Thinkstock.

This book is printed on acid-free paper.

authorHOUSE®

The book is dedicated to My DAD

Satyabrata Mukherjee

FEYNMAN'S PROMISE
Amrita Mukherjee

He does not care. *What's the big deal? Why do people get angry so easily? A railroad mess up, six hours delay is something new in Indian railway system? Come on!!* He glanced like an irritated babysitter does to smudge faced toddlers to his co passengers who were almost in a mini riot discussing callus railway administration, stupidity of railway minister, hypocrisy and ultimately incompetence of ruling parties. Sleeves were rolled up, overactive Adams apples, gruff voices rattling and few banging on walls, quite a scene. He travels in this line three times a week and inevitably this happens twice a month and amazingly enough people always react in a way that it's twin tower collapse of September 11. Spoiled, mega sized kids!! Each gives him mild nausea. Too much drama.

He pulled out extra battery pack from his backpack and put the android in charge. Of course plugged earphones and looked at his screen. Instantly three windows opened, one WhatsApp, two separate messengers and one yellow phone message box. He pays extra money each month to handle and download large data load on the go. Trisha the Boston girl said *"Honey! where u been? hey I am home from wrk its 9 pmish...guess watt for dinner... helooooo ....guesss guess...yam yam yam ur favvy favyy thing.....ummmmm ...tell me??? Aha aha...."*

Overweight, fat, turkey, idiot! He cursed silently under his breath.

But typed.."*Baby I know... honey roasted chicken? and baked beans? Aww Slop slop ..ummm*".

The whatsapp window had a veiled burkha face with hot pink cheeks. *"Salam humsafar.....kaisa chal raha hai tumhara safar... hanh....ankhe bandh karlo ar soch lo ki koi tumhare sath chal rahee hai...uski uri uri zulfe ...anchal ki khushboo.. ehsas karlo meri Zan........You tube clip popped up " Ai mere....humsafar..ek zara intezaar"*.

DAMN, what an obsolete Jurassic park song! Absolute Nani Amma!!!. He wrote *"Safar me dhoop toh hogi... Woh chal sake to chalo"*.

The messenger was a video window, Kim the Vietnamese girl with a string lacy nightgown, popping on the pillow. Her pink curves bulge obvious over the pillow, a husky voice hissing *"Baddd mannn…u are Late..ee… I been waiting….sooooooo long. Where R U? I need U ..U U U….* His face softened. A naughty smile came up. This is his favorite window. He scripted lavishly. *Come on baby… yess… right there… AHHH….feels good ….UR Deee best… don't stop.*

The unbearable heat, ugly compartment, slow webbing train, yelling passengers faded away. He was in a miracle land. He was enveloped with love, care, passion, attention and pleasures that he is been missing since childhood. His imagination was flying, senses were tickled, smiles were warm and real. He was eating dinner in a marble table with candles and lavender flowers with the Boston girl. She was bending softly to wipe the corner of his mouth with a napkin like Rani Mukherjee did to SRK in Kabhi Alvida whatever!

In his real life he mostly eats alone, junk dhaba food, wilted bad oil snacks and rotten peanuts that leaves permanent bad taste in his mouth.

He was riding camel back in Alhambra desert to Morocco with the burkha girl. In Oasis, he let her lie on his lap and recite the poems. Her long honey colored hair flying in sunny desert air, soft and subtle. He was feeding her dates, while she was licking his fingers.

He never had been this romantic with his wife. She would give him a dirty look and say "Pervert" with extra force on T syllable.

He was in a physical frenzy online with Kim. His whole existence had a whirlwind eight min exasperating liberation. He feels so happy and spent afterwards. Almost a glow. He never had it in his real life legal dark room rituals. He had to be careful, guilty and incomplete every time to keep it less traumatic for Leena.

The final text message box opened up and it was Leena. Focused, cold and precise. *"Take yr vitamins, and send one thousand Rupees extra to Tukai's hostel. And doctor said I need a chk up. B here two Xtra days next week, and don't chat with YR stupid chicks all NT for God's sake."*

He closed the phone windows. It was dark now dark outside. The train took speed and racing smoothly through marsh lands. All the rioting co passengers are half asleep. Dim lights dwindling from sooty ceilings. Peanut shells all over the floor, dirty curtains of two tiers. He was numb. He felt no emotion, He was just there siting inside his regular colorless life. Unwillingly he was breathing and living it.

Next day he had another bad news. Boss is visiting the sites. That means he has to work until midnight giving him service in the name of companionship. Hopefully he is bringing good whiskey this time. Last time he brought cheap Rum which smells horse urine. He gulped it down as if he was enjoying every stupid drop of it and smiled of course. That's why people liked him a lot. He does not complain. What's the point? That's not going to change anything. He stays cool and calm. Even ignores when Leena throws cups, plates and sometimes shoes at him in anger storm. He picks them up in trash gently. Gives her Benadryl to calm down and sleep. Makes tea for her the next morning. Sometimes she even says sorry which sounds like Hebrew/Latin. So unlikely for her.

He had to pick up Boss from Airport. Boss was polite but sarcastic, fussing about last month's report. Pushing him to go to Vizag for next weekend for a project. He smiled and said that will be awesome provided he can take the other Sunday off in Diwali. Boss said yes absently, without realizing that will make his total holiday ten days uninterrupted.

"Mindless idiot"! He cursed under his breath, in loud; he said *"Do you mind SIR if I stop here for Samosa…..they have some special samosas here with fried peanuts inside"*. Boss's dull face lightened up like vapor candelabra mercury lamp. Eyes glistening he mumbled *"You are the only one who can read my mind."* He smiled again. One of the meek smiles that he practiced since childhood. The one that makes him look like a lost boy with innocent damp hair on forehead. People's heart melts and they give away the guard for a lost little cute boy.

Over tea and samosa he showed Boss the pics of Boston girl. Introduced her as childhood friend, flourishing in America writing desi literature. Boss's reaction was instant and predictable. Wiped his lips with tongue and exclaimed she is cute a bit overweight though. He ignored boss's number five soccer ball size upper abdomen and agreed saying food habits in USA are notorious. Rest of the drive was easy. Boss was engrossed in more pics he supplied on his phone and was seriously talking about the prospect of Indo American literature. It was a good sign. So he may gently discuss the promotion with him after dinner with whiskey. He was buzzing definitely.

Next week he had to stop at Kharagpur at Tukai's hostel. She was not there so Sonia came down to say hello to him. Tukai's roommate has extraordinarily polished, cream like marble legs and although he never physically looks at the skimpy shorts she casually wears, he knows every strand of color and texture by heart. She makes him feel young and uninhibited again. He is more comfortable with her talking about hydraulic pump designs than Tukai. She said "Hello Uncle!" and gave him a light hug and he could smell the sweet sweaty deodorant, nicotine and fresh youth. In a whisk his college days came back. He shouted "SuRRRPrise…close your eyes". Sonia was startled but closed her eyes and he put the Chetan Bhagat's new best seller in her palm "Half Girlfiend".

Sonia was looking at him astounded and pleasantly flattered. Rushes of tight hugs followed with excitement *"Uncle!!! You are the greatest!!! OMG sooooo cool, how did U know? I like his books soooo much"*. This time he could feel there were no bra and the brush of rosebuds on his chest. He smiled and this one is the Alok nath style. *"I know your taste Beta; you are my second daughter"*. Sonia was in serious emotional trance and softly uttered *"Tukai is so damn lucky to have U…. Uncle"*.

"No, I am not". Tukai said with ice and venom in her voice. She came down the stairs to join them. Wearing big, dark glasses and flannel Pajamas. With an attitude of Nigerian soldier, she asked *"Did you bring the extra cash Mom told U"*. No hello, no hugs, no smiles, no thank you. He took a sharp breath in. This is the only weak point he has in this whole entire world. He can die willingly under those sizes six small feet of his daughter any day. He used to buy expensive red velvet shoes when she was a baby and never let her finger go off his own even in deep sleep.

So he ignored the insult. He smiled. Like Anthony Hopkins, a lost, sad dad in Mask of Zoro. And handed her the cash. He was not sure whether to pull out the chocolate wafers he brought for her. She counted the money and waved at him dismissal. *"I am late for class… got to move now"*. He stood there quietly. Both of the girls went up the stairs. Sonia looked back and winked before vanishing. He winked back. He knew she would do that.

Another train ride to get home. He feels tired and exhausted sometimes like travelling constantly between cities. He longs for fresh bed, his simple study with open window where he can see rain falling on nameless bush with tiny yellow flowers. His pet squirrels who comes to window to eat the morsel he saves sometimes for their unannounced visit. He missed the smell of Darjeeling tea from Leena's kitchen in rare afternoons brewed in a porcelain pot.

His phone rang again. It was Shuvo. His childhood friend. Usual slangs and calling him lucky, drenched, pseudo mule, Shuvo proposed instead of going home he should come to Calcutta. Rohan is coming from Dubai. There will be a get together at Mofongo Bar. He is going to be really a drenched mule not to attend. Somehow Shuvo likes him somewhere under his hard core promoter shell. Calling him pseudo and drenched mule asserts that. He knows and feels it in his own way. He said he will try.

Next call was from Leena. *Did he give the cash to Tukai? Usual policing questions. He gently proposed rerouting Calcutta plan. Leena hissed like a wounded snake. "Why not? Of course…U must get your fun with your drunk, hooligan friends; it's all about YOU and your pleasure. I am sick, your daughter is having final exam…just ignore, who cares? Go see half naked lasses in the stinky bar with your good for nothing, baboon faced, idiotic friends…who does not give a damn about you. At least if you could make money like them, I would not mind….a failure, complete black sheep with a weird family. Crazy mother, crazy son….burned my whole life in hell!!*

It poured on him. Like a muddy, splash of dirty water, molten lava quality. Sharply chosen insulting words, curses, yells, humiliations. For last twenty seven years he adjusted himself. Reshaped his concept of sadness, accepting it as a form of caring from a wise wife. Under his thick, slimy skin he learned how to hide each shrapnel comes with each word. Generally it does not bother him. But today something happened. A sleeping emotion started stirring up under his long lost self-respect. May be the mention of his mother. He had to send her to old home in the name of incurable insanity, to keep peace with Leena and in laws. Not that he is a devoted little mama's boy but Mom loved to cook rice pudding for him on his birthdays, with unknown dried flower petals. That smell and texture is one of the few things he could rejoice of his childhood. He never celebrates his birthdays any more, neither has he eaten rice pudding.

He closed the phone. Stood few minutes over the bridge. Busy afternoon was rolling downstairs with home going passengers. Loud speaker announcement, dust, setting sun created a strange canvas on which he was looking for his favorite color. Blue. He was almost suffocating for a little piece of blue sky. He will make it. He will get over this tightness on his chest. He could ignore the evil words about his Mom. But the whole sky was pale yellow, acidic like jaundiced eye of a dying liver patient. He dragged himself down the stairs. In a haphazard choice sat down on the first rickety bench he could find. The platform dogs surrounded him to say hello. Soft charcoal eyed, waving tales, hungry, brown angels. Slowly he took out the chocolate wafer packet he bought for Tukai. One by one he feeds them to the dogs. They were so happy. Making soft thankful moans, licking his toes, wagging tales like crazy. He felt calm and normal again. Since a boy, he loved to feed street dogs. After one hour he changed the platform along with his mind and took the train to go to Calcutta.

The bar was full and soft smoke spiraling with mixed smell of margarita and tequila. He filled his thirsty lungs with the smell of nicotine and pure malt scotch, must be Glenvitis. Makes him feel relaxed and spunky at the same time. He can do some wistful things in this air of temporary comfort. Thanks to NRI friends who offer the rare opportunity to splurge on expensive liquors to low profile desi classmates, displaying their wealth and success. Shuvo yelled from the corner " *RRREE bastard edike…..U are late*" They were all huddled in a corner. Pradip, Rohan, Shuvo, Peter,

Asad. Rohan grabbed a handful hair on his skull " *RRE chikna,,,,you still have hair, damn you, loookk at me, pura Ganja, Takla.* All broke in loud laughters, pushing each other with beer mugs. Asad gave him tight hug and said " *where u been…last saw u in WW II 1942*" and *Shuvo theatrically added* " Acting as blinking Lush Murda in yearly Drama", Another roar of laughters. He feels so precious. All his drunk, slang uttering thick friends,….. but they love him, they even remembered small little funny mishaps he did in some stupid school shows during his insignificant past. When he was a little human with interesting contradictions. He did not look like a fatigued cash machine then.

"Speaking of WAR", Peter added in a semiserious voice. "Things were damn scary in my last photo shoot at China border".

"A Be…. Shut up" Tu and tera Discovery channel. Maf kar yar.. We all having good time. No horror, gore details of your slaughtering madness". Shuvo snapped.

"RRE bolte de na…….Let him"….. Pradip, the peacemaker…put his palm on Shuvo's mouth.

Peter smiled and said " *Shuvo….its not about bragging my camera lens Yaar.. but thx about your dirty insights…..it was that the army is doing such a mess in Arunachal border. I went to this village which got burnt twice and mostly inhabited by girls who were raped by army jawans.*

"Ai stop….No Naki Kanna"…. Shuvo shoved Pradip's hand from his face… howling *"What do u expect? HUH?? you drop this poor Jawans in a F…. king triangle of Nepali Maoist, Chinese guerilla and Naga Rebels…. To protect your precious ass… in the name of national security… they will read Tennyson's poem?*

*"Shuvo …stop …that's not even an excuse"….*Rohan slammed down his mug. *"How ridiculous…is that the way you going to justify a rape???"*

*"Ok, Ok, everybody calm down…all are drunk… Let him finish"….*Pradip raised his hands up…..

"Exactly…thanks." Peter spoke again, *"among all the massacre, agony and pain, these days the area also is having earthquake, A monastery and a hospital got rumbled at the line of control, near Dambuk village, at the side of Dibang river. I was out there shooting and one day, I had to take a trip by motor cycle to the actual rumble. The most majestic ride in a motorcycle on the dry riverbed of Dibang River. I had to stop for chai pani in between, a place so small and unbelievable amongst all the Blue Mountains and open sky.*

There was this chai wala looked non Naga to me and he said he is actually from Goya, Patna, "Pet ke liye kya kya nehi karna parta Sahib?". Babu from Calcutta?

Yes !! he went to Calcutta couple times. Bariya City, Durga Mai ki dhum dham se puja hoti hai. *"Babu do you speak Bangla?"* Peter laughed, and added *"He probably got confused by my name that I could not be Bengali. Chaiwala told me there is the missionary camp used to be there, and a Calcutta memsaab used to work here with poor, destitute raped women. Some Christian church thing as you might know fifty percent in Arunachal are Christians."*

"Memsahib? Bengali?" Shuvo's face changed. He is been sipping vodka steadily.

He quickly licked his negroid lips with glistening eyes. *"Now I am interested. RRe gadha! Drenched Mule !! that should be the first thing to have come out of your VETKI mouth."*

Peter shrugged hopelessly. Shuvo and his fantasies. Pradip did another *SHHHH* hush to Shuvo.

Peter continued, Chai wala said *"Poor memsaab worked very hard babu! …. took care for the unfortunate women, everybody ijjat (respect) karte uski inha, Jawans vi darte hai usko Sahib. ….She fought with them to rescue the badnaseeb girls. Shernee (tigress) tha pura Shernee (tigress). But kiya naseeb!!! Memsahib got bimar Babu, Shuna hai Cancer, she is about to die here alone, no family, very sad. Lying alone in that broken hospital. She lost all her hair babu. By God aap jake thora dekhlo. May be you can help. May be you give sandesa (message) to family."*

"I found it fascinating. So I rerouted and went to see the damaged hospital building. And guess who did I found?" Peter paused….

"WHOOO" all five asked same time with same intensity.

Peter smiled and said *"Chitra".*

There was a brief ten seconds silence. Then everybody started talking in a confused flood of emotions. Asad : *"WHAT??? that skinny girl from station side road of our town?"*

Pradip: *"Chitra? Her dad was Christian, mom Bengali, had amazing long hairs?"*

15

Shuvo: "OMG horrible temper. She had high up nose, ignored us like we did not exist or some uncouth leeches like Romeos."

Peter smiled sadly. "Not anymore. She is reduced to skin and bones. Lost all her hairs. The poor mission folks were able to arrange a chemotherapy. Pathetically failed on her and she had horrible reactions. Some kind of lymphoma. Barely could recognize me. She was never married. Worked as a social worker in the mission. For last fifteen years alone in that God forbidden cold land. Under the breath of army, Naga rebels and Maoist. I dared not to take any picture. But same smile, unbelievably heartwarming.

Same old pride. "Don't tell Peter anybody, I am ok here. I am doing fine."

"What the hell!! Who cares? Why you giving me sad stories Peter on a fun evening?" Shuvo blurted. 'I don't give a damn, a flat chested skinny girl from past, let her die. Who told her to be Joann of Ark, rescuing woman in a horrid place?? HUH??? Bullshit, stupid….. strong head!!! That happens when you don't get a man in right age in right place in your body. Deprived, idiotic social workers, making us look like piece of joke, what right she has to do that, HUH??

He rose slowly but steadily from his barstool. Nobody noticed, as nobody ever imagined he would do such a thing. He grabbed Shuvo's neck, so tight that almost choked him, his finger white and stiff with anger, pressing hard. Shuvo started making audible gagging noise and eyes bulging out more in shock than fear. The bar man grabbed him from behind and pulled away. Everybody stunned, Pradip frantically screaming *"Let him go, you drunks…ENOUGHHH….* Finally he let him loose and stood up. Threw his glass as it shattered in pieces in the mirror. He did not say a word. Picked his bag and strode out in the dark, raining night.

He was walking alone pointlessly in the rain. He was feeling nothing else but a dull stabbing sensation at his heart, as if blood was oozing out in epileptic convulsions. Scattered pictures of a library room, filled with books, Chitra, sitting in the corner window table, her exquisite thin face, strange eyes with dancing lights, were coming back. One by one with new twist of torture. He was squinting his eyes. Why the memory hurts so much?? He used to go to Library to find his recluse in long summer vacation days. Mom was sick, mostly hospitalized. A strange disease after her untimely hysterectomy. He never understood. There was nobody home to cook lunch. He starved himself most of the time. He was tired eating alone in that cold dining table makeshift lunches of soggy sandwiches dad made before going to factory.

Chitra was always there. Studying books, later he discovered not textbooks but some strange books. He liked the way she was always engrossed, paid no attention to him or anybody, lost in her little world absentmindedly making small rings of her amazing hairs with rotational movement of her fingers. Some day she would have a little red plastic tiffin box and eating cautiously (no food in library) some yellow fragrant thing that make his stomach arch with hunger. So one day he pulled all his courage and walked to her table. She was reading a red book, a funny face on top something scribbled "Surely you are joking Mr. Feynman". She looked up and smiled. Said nothing looking back to her book as if she knew he was coming. After

little awkward moments he sat down, pulling one of the chairs and asked her about the book. She smiled again and pulled out her tiffin box, placed carefully behind an open book. He ate the last morsel of the halwa. She smiled again, Taking it away hiding in her bag. Then she stood up gathering her stuff, but the book. *"It's a book you must read"*. She said and walked away.

Next seventy two hours was blur frenzy for him. He absolutely did or rather could do nothing else but read that red book. Richard Feynman, the famous Physicist of Manhattan project took away him in a strange ride of Physics, passion, love, miracle and simplicity magic of life. He never read anything like such before. It was a pleasant shock he enjoyed every spark of it and felt like reborn. She did not come to the library for next three days. He was frantically looking for her everywhere. Bus stop, cafeteria, market, playground. She was not there. On fourth day she came late and sat right across from him and smiled. Suddenly the day was not cloudy anymore, the room lightened up, and invisible warmth of sunlight filled him with pleasure. *"So?" you liked it?"* She asked in an unsure voice.

He was pouring out. Could not stop talking about the book each line, each page, about Feynman's wife Eileen, her tragic death in Lymphoma, young love, dedication, unbelievable sad ending of their story. She was listening. Focused and quiet. A strange light was dancing in her eyes. Finally when he stopped she smiled again.

Then she said *"You see? Small things make differences. Feynman could have seen Eileen alive unless he had a flat tire in his car that day"*. They smiled together this time. They became friends.

That was the magic summer of his life. He spent twelve to fourteen hours each day with her in the Library or other small outskirts of the town. He carefully avoided all his usual buddies giving valid excuse of not playing soccer. They spoke about everything and sometimes nothing. Just taking silent walks in deep woods under huge canopies of trees and silvery cobwebs and cricket noise. She had strange topics, unexpected, sudden but silly sometimes. She confided him being deeply in love with a Russian storybook character Pavel Korchagin. In her wildest dream she walks with Pavel in vast snowfield of Siberia. Travels with Pavel in a night train, may be transcontinental railway berth, so close that their eyelashes touching. She was so different, so precise, so meticulous describing her dreams. Unknowingly he became a part of it. She always had some little snack or fun food with her. A piece of candy, small cold cucumber sandwich or Glucose biscuits. He loved her foods. He was never hungry around her. Gives him comfort he never got at his home. And the best part was he can brag about any cock and bull story, nagging about something worthless, she would listen quietly. The dancing lights in her eyes would tell she does not believe one word about it, but she is listening. She cared.

Strangely enough they were not lovers. Somehow it was never physical. There was a silent courtesy, respect and fellowship between them. A strong line not to be disturbed or to be crossed.

She never giggled or flustered, never wore short dresses neither painted her nails. Totally oblivious of her womanhood. The only thing was a bit distracting….. was her hair. Like soft monsoon clouds in wavy curls, dark and heavy with rain. Mostly tied with a lavender ribbon, loose ringlets flying around her perfect thin face. He struggled hard to stop his hand not to EVER touch those ringlets. He said "NO" many times to himself and feared to break the precious relation on just over some stupid ringlets. Sometimes she would stare at his neck for a bit more brief seconds than necessary and one day she admitted she was watching the cute blue veins while he was drinking water. His heart jumped to his throat, he was in total loss of words and started talking nonsense about some totally non relevant topic like voodoo practice of South African endangered tribes.

In last week of summer she did not show up four days in a row in the library. He felt like an orphan, lost, hungry, and deprived. He bitten his fingernails to an extent that almost nothing left to call as nails. He got trapped in one of the day match of soccer as got spotted by Shuvo. He badly sprained his ankle and had to lie down in bed with a mock plaster and horrible paste of home remedy tamarind and Chun (calcium powder). He was restless like a magpie bird, fidgeting over the solid, black prehistoric phone. Each time he dialed her no, a gruff inhibiting cold male voice responded "Hello". He hanged up as quickly as if he touched a hot iron and wished he could just vanish in thin air. On fourth day he could not take it anymore. He limped his way to her house. House looked a bit strange as all the lawn chairs were gone, and the blue fiat was not there in the driveway. The Gurkha at the gate informed they just left for station to catch the train to Calcutta. *Choti memsaab bimar. Need special doctors. Kab laut aye? kiya jane?* He ran or dragged pathetically rather on his limp leg and managed up to station. He pulled all oxygens in the whole world to hike up the thirty two steps in the over bridge to catch the right platform and then he stopped for a deep breath. Only to find the train started rolling like an unkind black elephant crashing and thumping on his unknown secret garden of lavender lilies. He stood there. Watching in disbelief how the train took away the most precious moments of his life with sad whistles and fumes. May be it was the coal dust or tear that made his eyes burn.

He could not remember what he exactly did in next few days. School opened after the break. The team had a semifinal practice. His Mom came home from Hospital, Shuvo got a new moped bike which all the boys took turn to learn riding, The River started swelling up with the threatening of flood. Monsoon continued with heavy downpour. It rained all day, like his heart never stopped bleeding silently, drop by drop. He never knew something can be so piercing like a fine sword dissecting his feelings so quick and precise, that he almost felt numb. A strange loss, emptiness like there is nobody in the whole town to talk anymore, to share his days, or just to look at. He felt so cheated, angry and helpless. He could not extract any news from anybody about her. She left no clue, no trails behind. The whole family was gone with her. She did not have any significant friends that he could tap. He visited her house every day.....with small hopes that may be she is well, came back, sitting in the lawn chair. He make sure he reserved always the window table in the library that may be one day he will just find her....sitting...absently playing with her ringlets....her face will light up with that incredible smile when she will see him. Never actually happened.

The night before last day of his final exam, he was late at Library. It was almost nine PM and most tables were empty. He was desperately going thru the integrals and cursing himself not practicing them before. He was tired, behind in each calculation, hungry. Lights were dim and it was only fifteen more minute grace time he got from the old librarian being a stubborn regular there. He could not take anymore. He slammed the folder close and dropped his head down on the table for few seconds. He felt a soft touch on his collar from back. He sprung back like a leopard does in the smell of blood. May be it's her.....he whispered *"Chitra??"*

The librarian was standing there. Thin old man with a kind smile. *"Are you ok my boy? You look terrible, exhausted....go home....and who is Chitra??"* He mumbled half inconclusive words shyly. He smiled and said *"Oh that thin girl used to study with you. I see.......I totally forgot. She left something for you one month ago, the last day she came here alone, she was not feeling well, left early"*. He stared at him in complete disbelief. Followed him staggering with his book bag up to his office. He took out a small, crumpled, brown paper bag and handed him. Inside, there was a small red plastic tiffin box full of dry nuts and raisins and a red book, the Feynman's book with the immortal story of Eileen and her being sick at a tender age. On the first page it was scribbled…in slanted lines… *"Never go hungry and no flat tires if I ever get sick. Smile. Chitra"*

They closed the library that day fifteen minutes late. It was pouring outside in torrential rain and thunder. The librarian saw the lost boy walked away in the rain, holding the book tightly to his chest. It was strange the way he was walking as if he found a new address. Out there he had his mouth full of those nuts and raisins, he was eating ferociously as with each bite he was trying to savor her last presence, the feelings left behind. He wanted to engulf it inside, not a piece could left stay behind. He was grateful that it was raining so hard that nobody could see how his face got washed with warm eye water too. He was consoled in a strange way. He had an answer to his prayers. He knew what to do….can never break that promise… had to be there with her….if that day ever comes….somewhere in the eternity. *He can't have flat tires….has to keep Feynman's promise.*

He did not remember how long he was sitting in the broken bench in that half dark park. Night elements were suspiciously rounding from safe distance around making sure whether he is a drug or flesh seeking entity. Rain stopped and a loose air with smell of burnt cigarettes and stench stolid river water was flowing. His hairs ruffled. He thought about the ringlets, those cloud like soft black hairs Chitra had. And then Peter's description of skin and bones. A dirty hospital bed, in a faraway land with a pale dying face, shriveled, hairless…suddenly his stomach wrenched and he bent down on his knees vomited helplessly. Acidic yellow water came rolling out with smell of whiskey and spilled all over on his trousers and black bag. Before he could wipe himself clean, the phone came alive. With slimy, vomit stained finger he punched the passwords. In the messenger window it was Boston girl. She chirped happy *"Hey hungry howey……where are u? Aww I am cooking again, chicken pot pie… yammy…with carrots and leeks. Will serve with a dollop of sour cream"*

He typed slowly *"I am sad….."*

She was silent for few seconds then the screen blinked *"Helooo! why???"*

He wrote *"A very dear friend from child hood dying in a far land……I promised …..long time ago…if that ever happens I will go…but it's silly…..it was twenty seven years ago….. she probably never even expecting me….and…..it's just impractical….maybe I'm just too* drunk…..but it just ….haunting me…..why I even came to Calcutta today…why I met Peter….why I came to know about her?"

Typed word came up "So you won't go?"

He typed "I guess not, I shdnt….it will be melodramatic…..nobody will understand… and U know what to say to wife and kids? Where I am going? Naww! that's ridiculous"

She typed "True! U get permission from your wife every breath U tk….I am damn sure"

"What d y mean?" He typed.

Screen blinked "You darn know too well what I mean. And I know too….under yr everyday sweet words u think I am a fat American cow….eating cream cheese 24/7…. but let me tell you my brain cells are not that fat. I can see you crystal clear, hopping in five different chats every night, cheating YR divine wife in every possible on line way, and splurging on your fantasies….and last thing you can do, stop making pathetic surreal excuses for not going to see your ill friend… u know what…you are the worst caricature of a stupid man I wld be seeing probably in an entire life time…..ZIIIS……amazing…."

He typed *"You are insulting me"*

She smashed back *"Goddamn it…YOU got that right…save my day…let me have little pride left in my mind about you….move your disgusting, skinny, good for nothing ass… and go see your friend……at least do something…that u might be proud while retiring and dying like a dried prune in an old home."*

The screen went blank. No more messages. He sat there soaked in his own vomitus, stench, and guilt. He hated her words. But at the same time a wry smile came to his face. She can do it. Nobody else can make him so angry and infuriated. At the same time can make him do stark impossible things that he would never do under ordinary circumstances. That fat Boston girl, cooking and eating all the time. Who ever thought she can spurt so much anger to him and each word showed how much she cares. His phone blinked again. This time it was a whatsapp msg. A phone number, for some Father DaSilva, Bright Beginning Church, Dambuk Village, Arunachal Pradesh.

"No worries, we fixed Subho at the bar. If not U who else….??? Safe journey…. Bravo". Peter typed.

He believed it now. It is a sign.

The Curio store manager looked in surprise. The green exquisite designed jade stone necklace was in his hand. *"These are not real stones; it's a fake necklace Sir. You said you are looking something for your wife."*

"This one will do". He said and reached for his purse.

The manager hesitated, putting it in red velvet case. Closing the lid he tried last time. *"I have real emerald chokers Sir, in case you rather take the real stuff"*….he irked.

He smiled and said *"I need to pay real price for that too right? Cant. In a budget now. Have to get plane ticket too."*

"Oh I see" the smile broadened in manager's face. *"You are taking her to go abroad? Aww that makes sense!!..I am sure she won't mind a fake necklace then?, Very thoughtful… actually smart Sir".*

He did not explain or protested. Took the red case and said thank you.

Outside on the porch he made the phone call. Few times the line broke. Faint… muffling sounds in the line. On fifth trial someone picked up the phone. He wanted to speak father Dasilva….a long pause….he was on hold…… The line got disconnected again. This time he tried seven times before the line got connected. A faint British accent with soft Ts. Father spoke. He introduced himself as Chitra's

29

distant cousin. *"But she does not want to see anyone. The lymphoma spread too far, we don't have too many resources….we tried… the first lapse of Chemo was successful… but it relapsed. She works too hard. Never rests. Goes alone in the border to rescue raped girls. Brings them back to shelter. Her cell counts low now. Platelets are falling. She is bleeding even with minor scratch. She is bedbound. Recently got horrible breathing issues, recurring pneumonias. Yes we don't have air conditioning here. It's a small church. We tried to send her away to a better hospital. She is stubborn. Said she does not have any one. Everybody loves her here. We don't have much medical care. We pray all for Chitra Memsaab. Yes…she does not have much time left….last visit the doctor from Dimapur said…matter of 2-3 weeks. Hurry up Sir. She cannot speak anymore…but she smiles. We feed her with straw."* He could not hear any more. Hung up the phone. Took the train to go home.

Leena was in shower, humming softly an old adhunik song. In her young years they used have separate Puja albums of upcoming new singers. It was so natural to have them along like lotus flowers and stunning blue sky of Puja days. She used to go with a puja offerings/thali in the local club wearing a magenta sari with soft peach lipsticks. In the misty, shy dawn lights he used to be there to accept the thali. The magnificent Durga sculptures, smell of incense, sheeulee flowers mixed with dew drops used to set the stage where two unsure hearts met with a spark of touch in a fraction of seconds while exchanging thali. She still savored the memory deep in her heart under all frustrations, anger, betrayals and bitterness. Last night brought back those magical moments. He was demanding and insatiable. Pain was mixed with pleasure as the ferocity softened the usual defense. He explored and won all lost territories in her long forgotten sensuality and at last emotion drizzled like soft morning rain. She did not wake him up. Softly made to warm shower of the other guest room. Happy warm waters made her feel new and she gently touched those bite marks on her neck with rare affections.

May be she will make those smoked Hilsa today wrapped in Banana leaves that he loves to death. She will not worry about cholesterol today. She was sliding in her pink housecoat that she rarely wears. She made sure she wore silk and lace under wears today matching dusty pink in color. She brushed her long hair and put a small kumkum bindi on the fore head. She did not become critical of her untimely wrinkles and dark circles under eyes. After pouring water in the house plants, she was still humming and making solemn vow that not for one brief second she will raise her voice or yell at him today. She will make it up and will start a new journey with him.

Leena brought out the exquisite bone china tea pot with daisy floral print from the shelf. She rinsed carefully with warm water and with a silver spoon measured two and half spoons of Darjeeling tea. She started the electric kettle to boil water and set the china cups and plates on the small kitchen table. She cut a small lily flower twig to put in the green vase that stands mostly empty on the kitchen table. As she lifted the vase, there was a scratch paper under something scribbled in his hand writing. Behind the vase there was also a sleek red velvet box. She opened it with unsure fingers….as the morning sun dazzled the fake green necklace. Thousands of glittering pieces of lights reflected on her astonished face, on kitchen floor, on the white waving curtains. She stood there in disbelief and read the note *"Got to go Arunachal for few days….my friend is sick, hope you like the necklace, forgot to give you last night, had to LV early, U R in the shower, TK care"*. Time froze in unreal eternity as tears were scared to roll down on her cheeks. The serene emptiness of the morning kitchen was worse than her hollow mind. The electric kettle whistled softly. Tea was ready.

The squeaky plane made thru horrible pockets as it was making its final rounds before grounding in the unwelcoming air hanger. The short ride from Calcutta was uneventful. Airhostess did not smile, although she has perfect curve at the left hip he absently noticed. He could not concentrate in anything……clutching that red old Feynman book and reading every lines …..probably, fifty fourth time in his life. This book is the only thing he possessed from his past. His only inheritance. Whenever he reads those chapters as "Lucky numbers" or "You just ask them" he was drifting in the past with Chitra. The lonely bridge they used to go and sit on top rails hanging their feet over the water. Feeding small chipped breads to fish and talking about life, possibilities. They never discussed disease, death or dooms of life those days. Everything was colorful, mysterious and possible.

The taxi driver promised that he will make to the bus stop on time where he has to take the bus to go to Dambuk village. There is an army checkpoint he has to cross and show his passport. Just because of the political unrest and being so close to China. *Babu is coming from Calcutta?? Reporter?? covering News??* He vaguely nodded his head. Did not give any specifics. Taxi driver was chatting…..*few months ago a news channel came here to do the story about the mad memsaab in Dambuk village…. rescuing the raped woman. But babu "memsaab sabko bhaga diya", said no tamasha!! go away.* He smiled inside. Yes! That's Chitra. Never went for cheap fame. The landscape was changing rapidly. Turquoise blue sky lined with silver mountains were in the horizon. Road side small village spots having Indo-Burmese looking women with colorful wool skirt, chubby faced babies, lines of bright paper flags, scattered markets. Soft rolling clouds over dark green juniper trees….he closed his eyes in pain…just used to be like Chitra's hair, soft, black, soothing.. with amazing ringlets. She lost it all….and he could not do any…she is dying alone…. bald, cachetic, cancer ripped her vanity, pride, look….He did not know…..He was busy doing what? smart things? Chatting with fictitious bimbos?? He could not find a place to stash his imaginary, unreasonable guilt.

The Taxi was passing through a small forest trail and slowed down suddenly, as couple people in local tribal cloth was standing in the middle of the road. The driver went down and came back with the bad news. *"Babu!! can't go any further, these people are saying bus is cancelled. Road sifted after rain last night."* They were speaking in local Deori not Hindi. So he could not understand. Apparently they were asking for rides. He said ok. Two of them came in the back, one in the front. Driver started the engine. Suddenly he felt the cold metal in his waist, as the left sided passenger wrapped his eyes with a piece of dirty cloth. He heard in panic the taxi door was opened and the driver were shoved out of the car with a ruthless hard kick. Door slammed back shut, car spunned round and everything went dark as somebody hit on his head with a heavy metal.

He was lying on the ground, face covered with blood. It's a small place cleaned inside deep forest besides the mountain gorge. Few scattered tents with ferocious barking dogs and strange people with rifles, torn olive uniforms and guns. They starved him, kicked on his belly and face several times in the process of taking away his passport. He could not understand their language. They have mixed features of Chinese and Burma decent. Merciless squint eyes. He was thirsty. They did not give him any water. Urinated on his face. He was lying there in complete disbelief. That he is actually taken hostage by this people. Are they going to kill him? Ask for a ransom? From who, what, why? His thoughts were running at thousand mile /hr speed.

They took away his belongings, moneybag, and phone. The pain is unbearable on his lower abdomen. He tried to move, only hounded by two ferocious dogs barking and licking his face. The guy in olive uniform shouted slangs and kicked on his back again. He arched in pain and cried loud. The guy opened his zipper and urinated on his face again. Suddenly he heard a commotion. Something happened. All the dogs started barking wild he heard a loud noise of a metal fan. A helicopter in the sky raving its metal fins. He saw in fear and horror the weird guy shoot the dogs, sprouted blood all over. Ran away with their belongings. Before disappearing in deep woods the guy turned back once and raised his pistol again to him and open fired. He could not move. Laying down there in blood, stench and mud in his face he felt the bullets hitting close to him in the ground. He saw the helicopter landed. A pair of heavy black boots running towards him, he lost his consciousness as the boots stopped few inches before his nose.

Major Surinder raised the glass. In return he smiled weakly. Saying cheers. He roared in his deep voice. *"You should thank the taxi driver, he reported to our army office. These Naga rebels are dangerous here, can take anybody hostage these days for passport"* They changes the picture and use it to cross China border. *But tell me why you want to go to Dambuk village. Why are u carrying passport?* He took time. With couple sips of the alcohol his brain started clearing up. He said about his unusual journey, his friend Peter telling about the monastery, Chitra, the missionary, saving poor raped women, …finally herself dying in sickness, Peter advising the danger of being close to border, …that's why he is carrying passport. Slowly the Major's face changed. His expressions hardened. *You came to see Chitra Memsaab? I see. Interesting!! Is she any relation?* He nodded, "No, a friend from childhood". "Girlfriend??" Major's sarcasm was obvious. He smiled *"I wish! but no! She was nobody's girlfriend, she was different".*

"Must be" Major's voice got unfriendly. *Making my Jawans look criminal to the whole world….. she must be different".* He grabbed his collar and dragged him up brutally from the chair and gritted like a wounded Lion. *"Listen Mr. Robin hood, this is my territory, I rule here. Don't ever think you can pull your funky Chitra card on me and make me nervous. I will report this as an encounter. Will shoot you like a fly and no damn soul will question".* He shook him violently and started pushing towards the gorge overlooking Dibang river.

He was feeling the unnamed tremor inside his stomach. Legs were weak and powerless, clothes torn, still smell like urine, what is happening now? Why is he here? Jeopardizing his perfect civilized life, leaving family and friends behind, playing with danger in each step for what? For whom? Somebody he knew twenty seven years ago??? Is he stupid? When did he become such a sentimental fool? He was losing control, his feet over the rolling stone and he could hear the roaring deathly river way down under the gorge. Leena's face came up, Tukai……they will never know.….he was shaking with fear. Major jammed him on the ground over the cliff and took out his gun pointed behind his head. Cold, ruthless steel ….knows no excuses. Major whispered *"Mr. Robin hood….you damn civilians….cute sensible people….do u realize that's how we danger our lives every day??? Do you?? Creeps?? under the gun of ruthless, mindless, reasonless rebels and enemies…….to save YR behinds…..every day…every single day of our life"*. He nodded, he could not stop, kept nodding, exasperated…..saying weak yesss!!!. *Major shouted " I can push you down right now and finish this melodrama…..but guess WHAT….. I have other plans"*. He closed his eyes. He felt he will collapse now finally. He can't take no more.

Major waved to his people who were standing behind and watching the soap opera in speechless silence. One soldier came with a roaring motor cycle. Major pulled him back and forced him on the rear seat of the motor cycle. He gave him back his infamous black bag, torn, covered with dust. He patted his back. *"Don't worry your passport and everything else we got in their tent inside this bag. Ride fast now. On Dibang valley no other commute is possible but the bike. So believe in your luck and Indian army. And the only reason I made it not look like an accident is I want you to meet your destiny. Tell your Chitra memsaab, we are not all monsters raping women. We are just regular army people with vices and virtues. So we know how it feels dying alone fighting enemies in a foreign land."* Motor cycle sped away so he could not hear his last few words.

He was just holding tight the rear bar of the powerful bike as it was passing thru the magnificent river bed of Dibang valley. Crystal green water cradled under deep blue mountains with soft white snow hats. Lush green waves after waves as valley unfolds its secret. The soldier was telling *him it's actually part of Lohit district, very close to Mc Mahon line of China. In month of July the Adi tribal have colorful festivals all over the valley where the Mishmi s dances with sticks to chase away evils. Missionaries worked very hard here in the past to stop cannibalism and hunting human heads. Peaceful people now joins in April month for Laho dance but due to recent earthquake this year's dance was not so good.* He was not hearing all but some. He was overwhelmed the nearness and imminence of the meeting. Is she ok? She will recognize him? What he would say? Why did he come? Does her eyes still have those dancing lights? Does she remember the promise? Feynman's promise? That she scribbled in that book before they parted?

Suddenly he saw the small shop in a bare patch of land in the middle of nowhere. He spoke up loud telling the soldier to stop. As they stop he spotted the chai wala. He ran in frenzy and asked about the village. Chai wala looked at him like he is an astronaut walking in regular ground. His surprise changed soon in dismay. *"Bari der laga diya Sahib, she not well, last we heard its matter of one or two days. She is vomiting puss and blood. She passes out, not eaten anything in last ten days. Jaldi karo sahib. There is a shortcut behind this valley that you ride and there is a little bamboo bridge you have to cross".* He turned back, gave no excuse to the soldier, took the motorcycle key and kicked the brake. The bike sprang like a smooth leopard with eighty five fluid muscles and disappeared in the half traced, wrecked narrow path, deep in the woods. In his dull, insignificant life this is the only thing he always felt confident about. He can drive motorcycle on a rope.

It was a strange, pale afternoon in Dambuk monastery. Father DSilva came to see Chitra. She is almost in a coma, shriveled like a dry flower in the small white bed beside the window. Afternoon sun softly touching her hairless head and swollen neck with peach glow. She turned left and clutched something under her elbow. The small, rickety bed side table has morphine injection ampules in a pathetic aluminum can. Her pain is not so bad this afternoon but pulses are so faint. Father looked at the socketed eye and pale face of that brave woman. She had so much life, so much energy, that head full of wild black hair, she used to tie with a lavender ribbon. Why God did this to her? He sat down beside the bed. May be this is his last prayer for her. He closed his eyes. *"Dear Lord, help her go see thy kingdom, ease her pain. Consider her my Lord as she saved so many lives"* he murmured….suddenly she moaned in pain….Father stood up looked under her twisted elbow. *"What is it my dear?"* then he saw it…it was an old, half torn red book….a story by some Feynman??? Father tried to gently dislodge the book. She made a violent animated sound to pull the book back. In commotion the book fell down wide open on the floor, as father picked up it again. There was a yellow, half torn photograph inside. *A teenager boy standing under a tree, surrounded by couple street dogs, feeding biscuits. Father felt the presence, a force, something powerful coming from nowhere to meet this fearless angel, to say farewell, to keep an unknown promise made long ago in the past. The ground was shaking.*

He heard the loud noise and was thrown out in front of the bike as he saw the tire burst and horrible black fumes came out. Suddenly he realized he is about to lose it this time.

No trick, no shortcut, no round about is going to work. *He had the flat tire* that he was promised not to have. It's over. He rolled down few yards to avoid the impact of his fall. And among deep wood, lime stone rubbles and twisted creepers he saw the bridge. A rickety bamboo one. The Dibang river was flowing with roaring, thousand horse like force under. He crawled with all tenacity he had left in his wounded, tortured, tired body. He would put his last drop of blood. He is not going to let it slip at this point. He came so far. The bridge was slimy, horribly unstable under his feet. Some wood partitions were missing. Some strong winds almost blew him out of balance. *He hunched like an embryo and started moving like a caterpillar over the bridge. He was not questioning anymore why he is risking every bit of his existence. He was unusually calm, focused as he feels the nearness, he feels her close by. He can do it. He can do it.*

Suddenly he heard the birds started crying loud on top of the woods. Some thing was shaking. Before he realized a huge stone started rolling down the hills. Earth was shaking water gushed in tremendous turbulence blinding his body, trees falling, grounds shifting, he felt the bridge was slipping. Bombastic lava exploded on the other side as it tore him from the bridge, throwing up and thrashing in the gorge. *He saw the huge root hanging in front him, with a strange lavender orchid, the same color she used to wear in her hair.* He grabbed the root with all his force and cry out loud her name for no reason. He was thrashed back in the mud on the other side as the retracting root and he saw the bridge broke in pieces like a cheap toy behind him under the roaring river.

The shaking was over. Everything was strangely quiet. Fumes and destructions were all over. Among the deadly canvass a yellow acidic rain was crying silently. A group of brown barking deer were hiding in the bamboo tree bushes nearby the landmark of Dambuk village 1 mile stone. The stone broke into pieces, but still readable. The baby deer was scared as it saw the strange mud soaked figure, crawling and rolling and finally getting up and running like a ghostly object, thru the destroyed paddy field, towards the Dambuk village. *Mud and dirt were all over it settled like cake, smelling rotten like old habits, guilt, perversions, dishonesty, but the acid rain washed some part of its head and face.*

He almost looked like a human.

END

ABOUT THE AUTHOR

Amrita was born as a fourth daughter of an engineer in a small industrial town of Durgapur, West Bengal, India. As she lost her father at a very young age, she grew up in an unconventional all women household of 1970's patriarchal Indian society.

Her passion for art and literature bloomed in those early years when she was studying Botany, with Biochemistry major at Santiniketan, Visvabharati.

She came to USA at tender age of twenty two as a student at The George Washington University, School of Engineering and Applied Science and completed her MS in 1997. Her career started as a System Analyst at General Motors/EDS.

Fate took its evil turn and at a critical juncture of her personal life, Amrita embraced Medical School at an advanced age. She passed with flying colors with best research award with the graduating class of 2008 from NSUCOM/ Florida.

Today Amrita lives in Orlando, Florida, being a dedicated Physician of homeless people in an underserved community. Amrita loves to go to mission trips in places like Peru and Africa. She has a daughter and her husband, who is constantly supporting her personal and professional development.

Amrita writes her stories, amazing milestones of her past, that she crossed as an Indian female immigrant in a foreign land and hopes that it will inspire many to fight their odds and enjoy the magic of survival.

Please send your thoughts and suggestions to AUTHOR at Amritascreativity@gmail.com.

Printed in the United States
By Bookmasters